THE INFLATABLES in SPLASH OF THE TITANS

DIVE INTO THE DEEP END
with more inflatable adventures!

THE INFLATABLES in SPLASH OF THE TITANS

By Beth Garrod & Jess Hitchman
Illustrated by Chris Danger

Scholastic Inc.

For my big sister and our times at Six Flags Atlantis —JH

For Chris, the Rock to my Lynn —BG

To Caitlyn, Heather, and River McDaniel —CD

ISBN 978-1-338-74902-1

10 9 8 7 6 5 4 3 2 1   23 24 25 26 27

Printed in the U.S.A.   37

First printing 2023

Book design by Stephanie Yang and Kay Petronio

Chapter One
One in a Melon

Everything *looked* completely normal at the Have a Great Spray Water Park.

But there was something unusual in the air. And not just Watermelon practicing her triple pump.

LOST & FOUND

2

3

But if Have a Great Spray is closing, then it's finally time for . . .

The Air-lympic Games!!

GOLD

10 10 10

I've been waiting my whole inflata-life for this!

4

Training every day has been worth it! This ball is ready to crush some Pineapple butt!

Wait. Did you say Air-lympics? TOMORROW?! But I haven't perfected my cheerleading routine!

Gimme a W, gimme an A, gimme an R, gimme a T.

Um. I don't think that's how you spell Watermelon?

And I haven't had time to finish my banner!

WATERMELON IS A CHAMPION

Good thing I had time to invent the ultimate training machine with ten mellion settings. Perfect for some last-minute practice!

Wow!

With inflata-pals like you, I really think I can win The Golden Pump!

THE AIR-LYMPIC TROPHY (ALSO KNOWN AS THE GOLDEN PUMP)

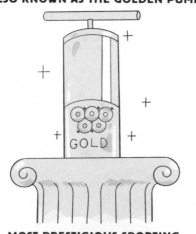

GOLD

MOST PRESTIGIOUS SPORTING TROPHY IN THE INFLATA-WORLD

This calls for a celebration!

Splaaaash down!

Sorry, air-migos. I've got training to do!

Don't you just love being a spectat-air? So much more relaxing.

Totally. Being sweaty doesn't fly with me.

Extreme spelling bees are fine. But the Air-lympic Games? C-O-U-N-T me out.

8

Bunch of inflata-wimps! I'll be defending my fifty-year title as Weird Weightlifting Champion. That refried has-bean Nancy the Nacho better watch out!

Don't you think you've done enough training, Watermelon?

Never . . . enough! Can't . . . let . . . Pineapple . . . beat . . . me . . . again!

9

PREVIOUS PINEAPPLE CRUSHES

THE N.B.AIR FINALS

TOUR DE PANTS

THE SUPER BLOW

WOBBLEDON

If I want to win, I need a good night's sleep.

But I'm too pumped to sleep!

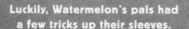
Luckily, Watermelon's pals had a few tricks up their sleeves.

And then the pig said, "Not by the airs on my chinny chin chin . . ."

Hush, little melon, don't you cry, Donut's gonna eat a blueberry pie.

Unluckily, their tricks were *almost* Watermelon-proof.

But with seconds to go, Watermelon finally fell asleep.

BEEP! BEEP! BEEP! THE AIR-LYMPIC GAMES START NOW! NOW! NOW!

11

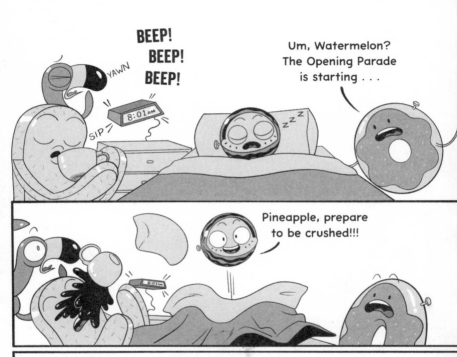

BEEP!
BEEP!
BEEP!

YAWN

SIP

8:01 AM

Z Z Z

Um, Watermelon?
The Opening Parade
is starting . . .

Pineapple, prepare
to be crushed!!!

WATERMELON'S VERY IMPORTANT AIR-LYMPIC STUFF. AND SOCKS.

Don't just stand
there! Let's go!

Welcome, inflata-viewers from around the world, as we count down the final seconds to the start of the Air-lympic Games, the most competitive day in the flata-calendar! I'm your host, Casey Dilla!

CASEY DILLA, THE CHEESIEST INFLATA-HOST IN TOWN

13

NEMESIS (NOUN): ARCHRIVAL, ENEMY, OR FRENEMY

WALTER S. LIDE VS DEODORANT

FLAMINGO VS BAD AIR DAYS

DONUT VS EMPTY PLATE

INFLATABLES VS PORCUPINES

**PAWS AND CLAWS
VS GNAWS AND JAWS**

WATERMELON VS PINEAPPLE

 That prickly player might
look like an innocent fruit.
But something doesn't add
up with her pineapple rings.

15

16

17

21

TEAM PINEAPPLE

Get ready for your swan song, Flamingo!

Queen Swanicorn II

Claim to Fame: The most feared—and most pampered—bird in the water park.

Goal: Always having more cup holders than Flamingo—or anyone else!

I'm gonna MASH you, Cactus!

Avocadon't

Personality: Mean, green, and totally two-faced.

Philosophy: Hates hugs, but hates Cactus more.

Donut, get ready to get dunked. Or tickled. But probably dunked.

The Fickle Pickle

Known For: Changing her mind. All. The. Time.

Biggest Regret: Donut once ran rings around her, so now she's on the warpath. Or not.

Nancy the Nacho

Best Quality: Fully loaded with hot takes and cheesy jokes.

Motto: I'm Nacho friend.

It's CRUNCH time, Lynn!

Gulp.

THAT'S what a nemesis is.

Chapter Three
A Sinking Feeling

After the Opening Parade, well, opened, the inflata-pals took a break to regroup.

So . . . you know when you were on TV talking to Pineapple?

Yeah . . .

And . . . you know when you said "Team Watermelon"?

Yeah . . .

Yeah, that was just a big joke. I would never make my inflata-buddies do anything they didn't want to.

Phew! I'm too smart to sweat.

I'd rather chill out. Especially if there are ice pops involved.

And I have a LOT of allergies . . . including an allergy to exercise.

No big deal. I'll just try again in ten years. What's 3,652.5 days anyway?

WATERMELON'S MOTIVATION BOARD

TODAY IS THE MOST IMPORTANT DAY OF YOUR LIFE!

YOU CAN DO IT!

IT'S BALL OR NOTHING

GO WATERMELON!

DREAMS DON'T WORK UNLESS YOU DO!

TEAM WATERMELON

SHIRTS

Are you serious? But what about your allergies? And your ice pops?

Smart move, water-wimps. I've heard my sporting hero, The Rock, is presenting The Golden Pump, and I'm ready to destroy the competition if it means getting one-on-one time with that hunk of hot air.

HONK HONK!

Whoa! Who are THEY?

They're the Air-lympic Games judges. Any rule breaking or arguments are settled by their decisions.

Susan Swim Cap

AIR-LYMPIC RECORD HOLDER:
Long-Distance Flip-Flop Fling

Known for: Pumping everyone up

Most Likely to Say:
"I believe in you (yes, you)!"

Surprising Fact: Can play the theme
tune to *Jaws* out of her air hole.

Gary Goggles

AIR-LYMPIC RECORD HOLDER:
Hot Tub High Jump

Known for: His 10,000+ goggles collection

Most Likely to Say:
"Do my goggles look big in this?"

Surprising Fact:
Has a house just for his goggles collection.

Simon Towel

AIR-LYMPIC RECORD HOLDER:
Previous winner of . . . nothing. But
he owns every TV channel, so here he is.

Known for: Deflating dreams

Most Likely to Say: "This water is
too wet! Can someone make it drier?!!"

Surprising Fact:
Discovered the Beach Ball Buoys.

Those judges are too cool for the pool.

But why are they holding up those signs?

That's how they let you know their decisions.

ALL JUDGES' DECISIONS ARE FINAL

INFLATABLE CHICKEN =
ALL OKAY. IT WAS IN THE RULES. NO FOWL PLAY.

INFLATABLE SAUSAGE =
THE WURST. YOU'VE DISGRACED THE WHOLEAIR-LYMPIC GAMES, AND PROBABLY YOUR FAMILY, TOO. YOU ARE DISQUALIFIED AND ARE NOT EVEN ALLOWED TO GET A LIMITED-EDITION BASEBALL CAP ON THE WAY OUT.

AIR-LYMPICS EVENT SIGN-UP

SPIKEY SLALOM   SLIDE-~-DIVE   AIR-RAISING WRESTLING   WEIRD WEIGHT-LIFTING   TRI-AIR-THLON

Let's flip a coin. Heads or tails. First to get tails takes on the Spikey Slalom.

HAVE A GREAT SPRAY
WALTER S. LIDE
2022
S. LIDE
WALTER TOKEN

HEADS

HAVE A GREAT SPRAY
WALTER'S BUTT
2022
WALTER TOKEN

Noooooooooo! TAILS

Chances of survival?

I'll tell you later . . .

START

Time for our first event. Bur Aid on standb

FLAMINGO

Favorite color: Pink

Butt tattoos: S.T.A.R.

Cup holders: It's what's inside that counts.

Fear of failure and spikey slaloms: Very high

QUEEN SWANICORN II

Favorite color: Rainbow

Butt tattoos: Ask me about my cup holders instead.

Cup holders: Count them—EIGHT.

Fear of failure and spikey slaloms: Low—let's go, beaky!

START

May the swan with the most cup holders win.

Chapter Four
3-2-1—BLOW!

35

And the racers are off to a speedy start!

WhereamI whoamI pleasedon't letmepop!

If he wins, Team Watermelon could go straight to the top of the leaderboard!

You've got this, inflata-dude!!!

Is it a good sign Flamingo's upside down?

Whatever happens, no one tell him about all the pop-stacles in his path—he'll panic even more!

SPIKEY SLALOM MAP

The first medals are up for grabs! But one wrong move and our intrepid air-thletes could get popped for good . .

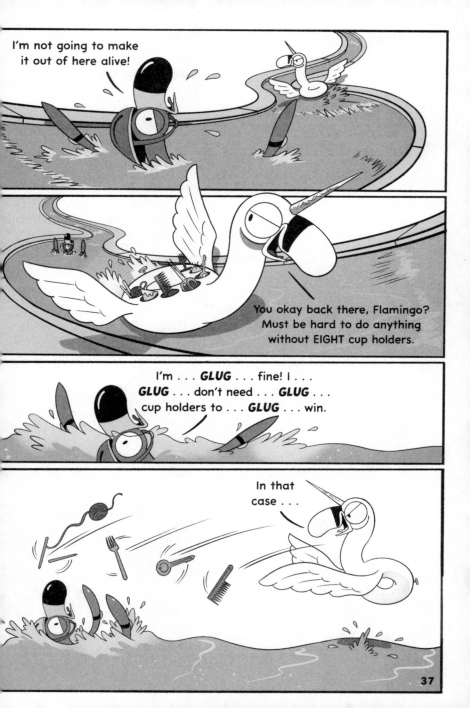

WOOOSH
WOOOSH
WOOSH

Brutal, but not against the rules! Could we soon be saying a fondue farewell to the fearless Flamingo?

He's sinking!

And he's still got the Toothpick Terror Tube to get past!

Right now I don't even care about winning. We need our pink pal back in one piece! We have to do something, and fast . . .

Flamingo! We believe in you!

HANG TIGHT, BUDDY!

TOOTHPICK TERROR TUBE

DEATH DROP
YOU DEFINITELY DON'T WANT TO GO THIS WAY!

39

41

Chapter Five

Do or Dive

I'm never moving again!

Bingo, Flamingo! That was enough drama for the next fifty years!

But that was just the first event!

We're at the top of the leaderboard—just where I dreamed we'd be!

Oh. I dream of floating in custard.

And I think we can stay at the top! I've analyzed the events and found my perfect match!

The Slide 'n' Dive!

SLIDE 'N' DIVE

THE SLIDE 'N' DIVE: EVENT RULES

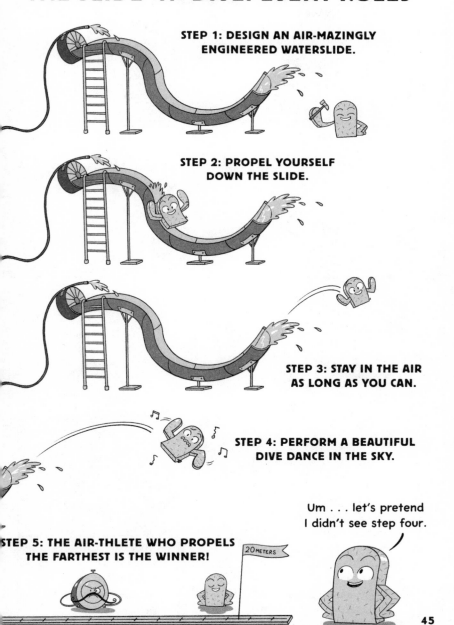

STEP 1: DESIGN AN AIR-MAZINGLY ENGINEERED WATERSLIDE.

STEP 2: PROPEL YOURSELF DOWN THE SLIDE.

STEP 3: STAY IN THE AIR AS LONG AS YOU CAN.

STEP 4: PERFORM A BEAUTIFUL DIVE DANCE IN THE SKY.

Um . . . let's pretend I didn't see step four.

STEP 5: THE AIR-THLETE WHO PROPELS THE FARTHEST IS THE WINNER!

20 METERS

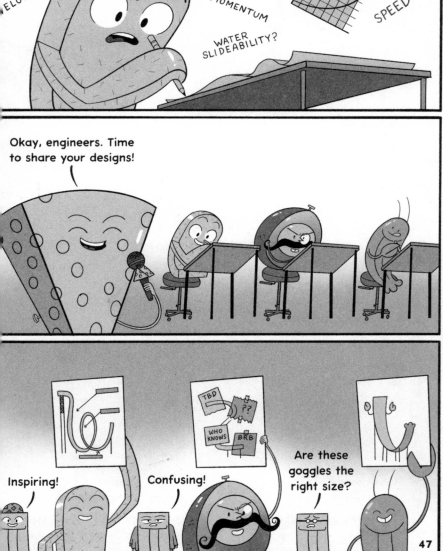

47

Now it's time to build those slides! But will they pop under the pressure?

SPOT THE DIFFERENCE

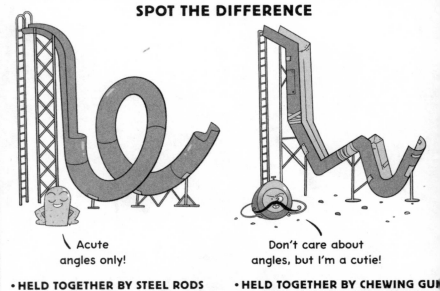

Acute angles only!

Don't care about angles, but I'm a cutie!

- HELD TOGETHER BY STEEL RODS
- CLEAN AND TIDY

- HELD TOGETHER BY CHEWING GUM
- COOKIE CRUMBS EVERYWHERE

48

Okay, it's time to Slide 'n' Dive!

You got this, Cactus.

Apart from the dancing bit.

You really don't got that.

But you've got everything else. So let's goooooo!

SHE'S CLEVER! SHE'S PRICKLY! SHE LEARNS THINGS VERY QUICKLY!

SHE'S CACTUS! HEY! HEY! CACTUS!

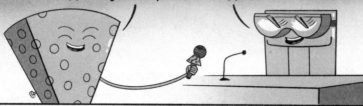

Cheese-whiz! What a result for Team Pineapple, right, Gary?

Oh, sorry. Was I supposed to be watching? Because Noah Noseclip just dropped a HOT new collection.

STANDINGS				
TEAM	GOLD	SILVER	BRONZE	POSITION
TEAM PINEAPPLE	1	1		JOINT FIRST
TEAM WATERMELON	1	1		JOINT FIRST
TEAM FANTASY			1	JOINT THIRD
TEAM FURNITURE			1	JOINT THIRD
YET TO SCORE	TEAM OCEAN, TEAM WEATHER, TEAM FOUR LEGS			
TEAM VACATION				NO SHOW

It's a tie at the top of the leaderboard! It doesn't get cheddar than this!

Don't worry, Cactus. There's something not ripe about Avocadon't, but we can still do this.

I mean, at least my cheerleading routines are getting better. I wonder who's up next?

It's . . . you!

ARRGGH!

53

DONUT

Fighting name: Stone-Cold Donut Donutson

Entrance music: "Love Is in the Air"

Finishing move: The Dirty Dunker

Ringside snack: Pickles

THE FICKLE PICKLE

Fighting name: Fickle "Who You Calling Sour" Pickle

Entrance music: "Air of the Tiger." Or silence.

Finishing move: The Gherkin Jerkin or the Jerkin' Gherkin

Ringside snack: Donut soup or donut salad

Oh, okay. Um, how soft is the material your nightgown is made from? Because *mine* is—

Stop talking about bedtime stuff and try one of these.

TRASH TALK IDEAS

KIDS PICK YOU OUT OF BURGERS MORE THAN THEY PICK THEIR NOSES!

WHAT DO YOU GET IF YOU CROSS A LIZARD WITH A CORN DOG? YOU!

YOU THINK YOU'RE SUCH A BIG DILL, BUT I'M GOING TO RELISH YOUR DEFEAT!

Sheesh, Cactus! I didn't know you had that in you.

Ding ding!

Enough talk, it's go time. In Brie . . . two . . . one . . . SNACKDOOOOOOWN!

58

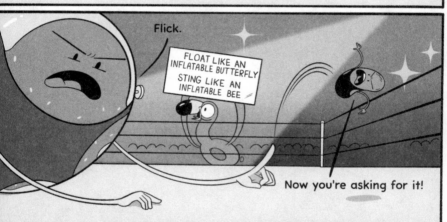

A TRAUMATIC HISTORY OF DONUT WEDGIES

I'm actually not impressed by either of them.

Donut did a cheerleading routine for everyone but himself.

I'll just have to make him a banner—and FAST!

CHEERLEADING FOR DONUTS

DONUT THE GREAT

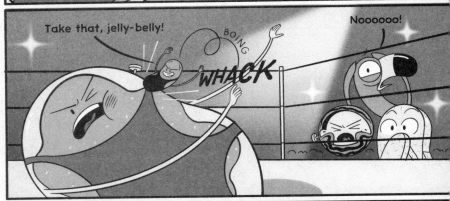

STANDINGS

TEAM	GOLD	SILVER	BRONZE	POSITION
TEAM PINEAPPLE	2	1		FIRST
TEAM WATERMELON	1	2		SECOND
TEAM FANTASY			1	JOINT THIRD
TEAM FURNITURE			1	JOINT THIRD

I'm so sorry, Watermelon . . .

SORRY I COULDN'T PUREE THAT PICKLE LIKE THE CONFUSING CORNICHON SHE IS!

Now *that's* how you trash-talk.

I think my consolation churros made it all pop out of me.

You've got nothing to apologize for, doughy dude. You did your best, and that's the most anyone can do.

And if Lynn wins the Weird Weightlifting, we'll be back to a tie.

IF Lynn wins??

We mean, WHEN Lynn wins.

Better. Everyone ready to start my pregame routine?

Do you think Nancy the Nacho has a pregame routine?

66

LYNN AND NANCY'S PREGAME ROUTINE

MEAL

POWER STANCES

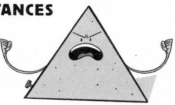

NAILS

TRAINING

Only two competitors made it through the qualifying event. Two of the most fearsome air-thletes on the circuit.

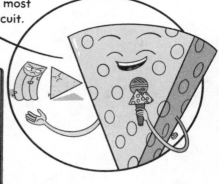

NANCY THE NACHO

Would most like to lift: ~~A ton of guac~~ cotton candy . . . if she's feeling strong.

Age: ~~Legends never age~~ Well past the sell-by date

Sports icon: ~~The Rock~~ Lynn

Loves: ~~Winning at poker~~ Losing to Lynn

LYNN

Would most like to lift: The Rock

Age: Timeless. (Judge's note: Lynn says 21. It's not 21.)

Sports icon: The Rock

Loves: Changing Nancy the Nacho's trading card

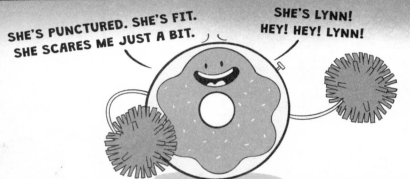

Lynn, you did it! The Golden Pump is so close I can almost smell it!

Are you sure that's not me you're smelling?

SNIFF SNIFF

No sweat. Crushing Nachos is what I was born to do. And anyway, The Rock is

Team Watermelon. You've been amazing. Now winning the Air-lympics all comes down to me beating Pineapple—just how it should be. Thanks for giving me the best chance a melon could ever have.

STANDINGS				
TEAM	GOLD	SILVER	BRONZE	POSITION
TEAM PINEAPPLE	2	2		JOINT FIRST
TEAM WATERMELON	2	2		JOINT FIRST
TEAM FANTASY			1	JOINT THIR
TEAM FURNITURE			1	JOINT THIR
YET TO SCORE	TEAM OCEAN, TEAM WEATHE TEAM FOUR LEGS			
TEAM VACATION				NO SHOW

It all comes down to this moment! The Tri-air-thlon. Three super-skilled events: Swimming Trunks Tightrope, Deep-End Dive Bomb, and Waterfall Scramble.

EVENT ONE: SWIMMING TRUNKS TIGHTROPE
INFLATA-DUDES BETTER TOE THE LINE (IF THEY HAVE TOES) TO BE FIRST TO THE FINISH.

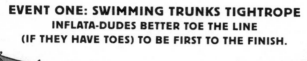

EVENT TWO: DEEP-END DIVE BOMB
HOW LOW CAN YOU BLOW? IT'S SINK *AND* SWIM IN THIS RACE TO THE BOTTOM.

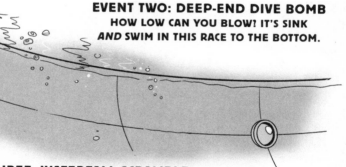

EVENT THREE: WATERFALL SCRAMBLE
THE WINNER IS UP IN THE AIR—WHO CAN SCRAMBLE TO THE TOP FIRST (AND AVOID DISTRACTIONS)?

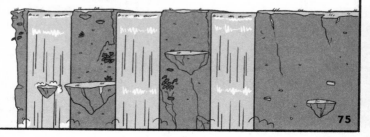

It's going to be quite the air-raiser! Winning means everything to . . . uh. . . . Wineapple. I mean Patermelon. Ugh! You know what I mean.

GO TEAM WATER-MELON

AVOCADOS ~~SWANS~~ ~~NACHOS~~ ~~PINEAPPLES~~ RULE!

WATERMELON

Air-gility: 2,500

Sporting motto: "It's ball or nothing!"

Most likely to be mistaken for: A bowling ball

Yum factor on a pizza: Low

VS

PINEAPPLE

Air-gility: 2,500

Sporting motto: "Not-winning is for losers."

Most likely to be mistaken for: A hairbrush

Yum factor on a pizza: High or low depending on who you talk to.

This is the moment I've been training for my whole life!

I'm going to beat that Pain-apple once and for all, and win for Team Watermelon and ALL the inflatables that have ever been forgotten, punctured, or used as household objects.

**HE'S RED, SHE'S BLACK, SHE'S GREEN.
SHE IS OUR SPORTING QUEEN!**

**SHE'S WATERMELON!
HEY! HEY! WATERMELON!**

**DON'T CALL HER HELEN!
HEY! HEY! NEVER HELEN!**

You guys are the best inflata-team a melon could ever have! Now I'm DEFINITELY ready!

BEEEEEEP! And they're off! Who will balance to victory on the Swimming Trunks Tightrope?

Say bye-bye to first place, you spikey, hard-to-cut fruit!

START

Remember your training. Just gotta roll with it!

START

FINIS

WOOOSH

Guess there are advantages to being spikey after all! You know what they say: It's really hard to balance an air-filled ball on a teeny-weeny rope made of swimwear.

Literally no one has ever said that.

80

ICE CREAM JEAN'S MISSING SCOOP

WALTER S. LIDE'S MISSING TOENAIL

2 FT

10 FT

12 FT

HELLO MY NAME IS FRED NESSIE

I ♥ LYNN!

20 FT

22 FT

FINISH

They made it look cheesey-peasy, but Watermelon clinched it! With one event left, and these two neck and neck, the Tri-air-thlon couldn't be closer!

GASP

HUFF PUFF

The Waterfall Scramble will decide the Air-lympics winner! Who will avoid the distractions and get to the top first?

Oh look, yet another adoring fan.

Greeting your fans already? You *schmooze,* you lose!

Woo-hoo! Training twenty-five hours a day every day was all worth it! I've finally crushed Pineapple!

FINISH

She did it! And set a new Air-lympic record!

I want to remember this moment forever!

CLICK

89

Team Pineapple wins the final gold AND The Golden Pump!

ALL I DO IS WIN!

I think I speak for the whole audience when I say . . .

GASP!

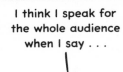
But I won fair and square!

STANDINGS				
TEAM	GOLD	SILVER	BRONZE	POSITION
TEAM PINEAPPLE	3	2		FIRST! AIR-LYMPICS CHAMPIONS!
TEAM WATERMELON	2	3		SECOND
TEAM OCEAN			1	THIRD
TEAM FANTASY			1	JOINT FOURTH
TEAM FURNITURE			1	JOINT FOURTH
TEAM FOUR LEGS				YET TO SCORE
TEAM WEATHER				YET TO SCORE
TEAM VACATION				NO SHOW

Try telling someone who cares. I'm off to have my trophy-carrying suitcase polished.

Inflata-buds, please don't say sorry. I couldn't be prouder of my team.

If there's one thing sports have taught me, it's . . .

Just say no to ice pops?

Don't underestimate a surprisingly long mustache?

Never trust anyone with more than one cup holder?

No. It's that sometimes inflata-life isn't fair.

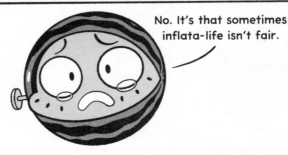

This is so sad.

Team Watermelon failed you.

And I don't get to meet The Rock.

Um, Watermelon, are you okay?

I'm fine. Totally fine. Just training for the next Air-lympics. There's no point in wallowing.

No point in wallowing?!

You've GOT to wallow a little!

But I don't know how to wallow.

I'll take it from here.

And I'll have some alone time with this.

THE ROCK

THE ROCK MAGAZINE

First, you have a big old ugly cry.

Boohoo!

Sniff.

Next you watch ten thousand episodes of your favorite show.

THE GREAT PECKISH BAKE OFF

planet mirth
WITH DAVID AIR-TENBORO

The Glidin' Girls

Then you crack open a tub of your favorite ice cream.

Or if you're in a water park that's closed for the day, you break into the ice cream truck!

Finally, you take a giant inflata-nap. Yawwwwn.

103

Face it, I won the Air-lympic Games. And destroyed a Watermelon along the way. So will you stop buzzing around? I have autographs to sign.

But . . .

But what, sprinkle-face? If that pumped-up Pickle overinflated Avocadon't, air-brained Nacho, and silly Swan (who will NOT stop going on about her seven cup holders) had been more careful, we wouldn't even be having this conversation.

Say that again, you lanky leaf head.

Did you just call me overinflated?

It's EIGHT cup holders.

I can't believe you call me pumped up. But also I can.

ENOUGH!

We heard EVERY word.

Do you like my new goggles?

It's not what it looks like!

Oh, it is. A Team Pineapple Total Meltdown! And I accidentally broadcast it, so the whole world knows, too. Sorry, not sorry. My goggles looked great in it, though.

109

Not the sausage!

Anything but the sausage!

Mmmm, sausage.

The sausage means . . .

 The Air-lympic Games reward air-thletes who push themselves to their limits *and* work with their teammates.

 For reals?! I thought I was here to show off my new goggles range. These have built-in wind machines for the ultimate glam look.

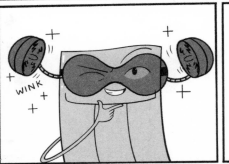

WINK

And one team clearly worked together better than anyone we've seen before. We have a new winner . . .

TEAM WATERMELON!

STANDINGS				
TEAM	GOLD	SILVER	BRONZE	POSITION
TEAM WATERMELON 🏆	5			FIRST! AIR-LYMPICS CHAMPIONS!
TEAM OCEAN		2	2	SECOND
TEAM FANTASY		2	1	THIRD
TEAM FURNITURE		1	1	FOURTH
TEAM WEATHER			1	FIFTH
TEAM FOUR LEGS				YET TO SCORE
TEAM VACATION				NO SHOW
TEAM PINEAPPLE	🥒	🥒	🥒	DISQUALIFIED FOR GOOD AND BROUGHT SHAME TO THEMSELVES!

Chapter Twelve

Swim When You're Winning

Winning this trophy feels even better than I thought it would. Because I'm sharing it with my best friends in the world.

119

AIR-LYMPIC CHAMPIONS: TEAM WATERMELON!

"FRIENDS WHO PUMP TOGETHER, STAY TOGETHER!"
—TEAM MOTTO

"OF ALL THE WATER PARKS IN ALL THE TOWNS IN ALL THE WORLD, HE WALKED INTO MINE." —LYNN

"THE BEST WAY TO BE A WINNER IS . . . TO THINK ABOUT DINNER." —DONUT

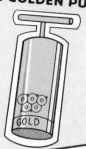

"FRIENDS ALWAYS GET YOU OUT OF A FLAP." —FLAMINGO

"SORRY, BUT A SAUSAGE REALLY ISN'T A SCORE." —CACTUS

"ANYTHING IS POSSIBLE WHEN YOUR RIENDS PUMP YOU UP." —WATERMELON

DIVE INTO ADVENTURE WITH
THE INFLATABLES

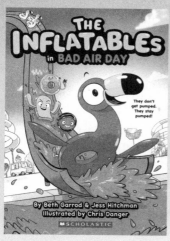

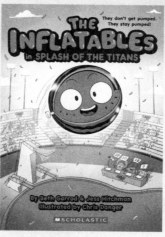

They don't get pumped. They stay pumped!

HOME BASE

YOUR FAVORITE BOOKS COME TO LIFE IN A BRAND-NEW DIGITAL WORLD!

- Meet your favorite characters
- Play games
- Create your own avatar
- Chat and connect with other fans

- Make your own comics
- Discover new worlds and stories
- And more!

Start your adventure today! Download the **HOME BASE** app and scan this image to unlock exclusive rewards!

SCHOLASTIC.COM/HOMEBASE